N ot nice

O pen oyster

P aint the pail

Q uilt a quilt

R ubber raft

S melly shoe

T rollusk tears

U sually unlucky

V ery vain vampire

W ash the walrus

X ray

Y our yellow yarn

Z ipperump-a-zoo

run

leap

hop

Table of Contents

climb

read

rest

crawl

fly

walk

Little Monster's Word Book

By

Mercer Mayer

fall

gb GOLDEN PRESS · NEW YORK

Western Publishing Company, Inc.

Racine, Wisconsin

dive

skip

tumble

slip

washboard

washtub bass

COUNTRY AND WESTERN BAND

bow

fiddle

kazoo

guitar

harmonica

five-string banjo

Cowboy Critter and his WACKY WACKY BAND

lute

drumsticks

batons

parade snare drum

baton twirlers

drum major

Music

7

roller coaster

County Fair

barn

silo

prize tomato

farmer

tractor

rooster

BUMPER CARS

cow

goat

sheep

horse

RIDE THE DONKEY AND GET YOUR PICTURE TAKEN

SHOOTING GALLERY

HIT THE BOTTLE

Teddy bears

pinwheel

milk bottles

camera

photographer

win-a-prize booths

cotton candy

8

Ferris wheel

TEST YOUR MUSCLES

bell

pinwheel

HOME MADE

cake   bread   pie

jams and jellies

mallet

Catch a Greased Kerploppus

RIDE A KERPLOPPUS MERRY-GO-ROUND

cotton candy seller

cone

ice cream

scale

foot-long hot dog

50 60 70 40 80 30 90 20 10 100

I WILL GUESS YOUR WEIGHT OR YOU WIN A BEAN BAG

TICKETS

weight-guessing trollusk

ticket booth

thunder lizard
(brontosaurus)

little
kitty cat

big kitty cat

This big bird is
called a pterodactyl.
I bet you a piece
of bubble gum you
can't say that.

That!

parrot

fish

goldfish

flea

cricket

hamster

white mice

10

The Great Pet Show

pet bat

pet flower

lizard

turtle

zipperump-a-zoo

pet snake

worm

puppy fydolagump

first-prize ribbon

pet shoe

puppy dog

pet-judging trollusk

(If you were the judge, who would get first prize?)

bone

11

Games

catcher's mask

catcher

bat

baseball?

ball

batter

mitt

pitcher

BASEBALL

bird

JACKS

jacks

CHECKERS

winner

loser

racket

checkers

checkerboard

birdie

net

BADMINTON

hoop

net

basketball

croquet ball

wicket

mallet

CROQUET

BASKETBALL

hider

12

pins

bowling ball

BOWLING

bowler

CARDS

football

catch

Who is right?

GUESSING

seeker

"it"

TAG

helmet

kick

target

shooter

ring

dart

MARBLES

IDE AND SEEK

DARTS

FOOTBALL

13

Things to Do With Paper

FOLD IT

hat

paper airplane

newspaper

CUT IT

paper doll chain

scraps (throw them away)

scissors

WAD IT UP

MAKE A MASK

MAKE A PAPER CHAIN

DRAW A PICTURE

crayon

pencil

ballpoint pen

Dear Bill, can you read yet.

WRITE A LETTER

paper with lines

clothespins

rope

string to tie it on

crayon

scissors (always be careful with scissors)

construction paper or cardboard

flashlight

paste

sheet

PASTE A PICTURE

MAKE A SHADOW-PUPPET SHOW

MAKE A FLOWER

stick

tape

heavy paper or cardboard

shadow puppet

Birthday Party

balloons

paper lanterns

egg-and-spoon race

punch bowl

egg

ladle

camera

sack race

party hat

noise-makers

candles

birthday boy

birthday cake

paper cup

party favor

bowl

plate

fork

Pin the Tail on the Kerploppus

shirt

tablecloth

presents

ice cream and cake

jigsaw puzzle

15

Weather

raindrops

hailstones

snowflakes

umbrella

HAIL

icicles

RAIN

SNOW

SUNNY

beach

lightning

FOG

THUNDERSTORM

TORNADO

WINDY

17

hot dog

hot-dog-snatching bombanat

tree house

bird

butterfly

lean-to

outdoor fireplace

CAMPING

flashlight

camper

backpack

canteen

sleeping b

hatchet

tent

sleeping b

anthill

ants

radio

picnic basket

cattails

rowboat

oar

Thermos bottle

frog

bench

cold milk

lily pad

picnic table

PICNIC

18

Summertime

kite

turning somersaults

kite string

HAY RIDE

fishing pole

can of worms

swimming trunks

bathing cap

FISHING

swimming suit

WATER SKIING

diving board

water skis

mast

sail

SWIMMING

BOATING

sailboat

pond

T-shirt
flag

snow
castle

ski lift

snow
shovel

SLEDDING

snow

top hat

sled

SNOWBALL FIGHT

gloves

jacket

sticks

ice
fangs

snowballs

BUILDING A
SNOW MONSTER

Thermos
bottle

hot chocolate

figure
skates

ICE SKATING

20

Wintertime

SLEIGH RIDE

ski poles

skis

SKIING

ski boots

icicles

ICE HOCKEY

hockey stick

mittens

hole

line

fish

snowsuit

bench

puck

mast

sail

boots

earmuffs

stocking cap

scarf

ICE FISHING

frozen pond

ICE BOATING

runner

Holidays

HALLOWEEN

witch

false nose

candy bags

TRICK OR TREAT

devil

skeleton

jack o'lantern

VALENTINE'S DAY

hearts

red paper

paper lace

paste

Make your own valentine!

scissors

THANKSGIVING

blunderbuss

roast turkey

pumpkin pie

Pilgrim

Pilgrim

turkey

EASTER

Easter-bunny suit

dyeing eggs

yellow

green

red

eggs

purple

chocolate bunny

jelly beans

Easter basket

22

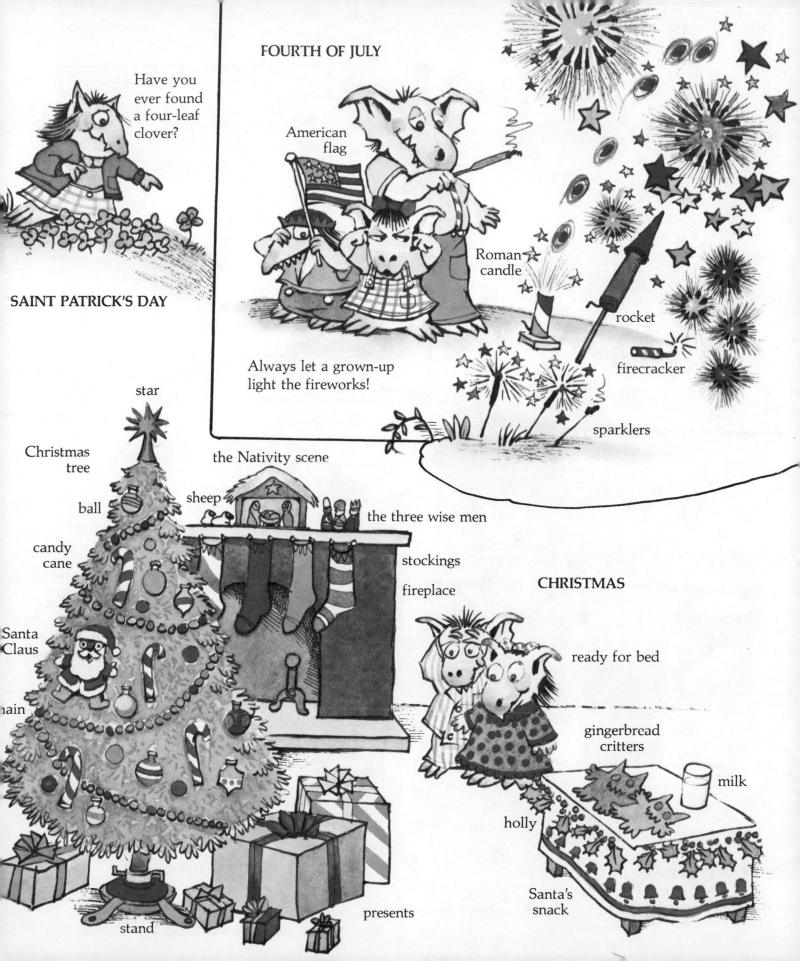

Have you ever found a four-leaf clover?

SAINT PATRICK'S DAY

FOURTH OF JULY

American flag

Roman candle

rocket

firecracker

sparklers

Always let a grown-up light the fireworks!

star

Christmas tree

the Nativity scene

ball

sheep

candy cane

the three wise men

Santa Claus

stockings

fireplace

CHRISTMAS

ready for bed

chain

gingerbread critters

milk

holly

Santa's snack

stand

presents

balloon

UFO

jet

tugboat

rowboat

oar

rubber horse

swim

canoe

submarine

by elephant

paddle

by wheels

diesel train

on horseback

EDGE of NOWHERE OR BUST

covered wagon

by feet

footprints

25

Moving Day

Have you ever rolled downhill in an empty moving carton?

chimney

roof

old radio

old picture frames

dress form

steamer trunk

ATTIC

LIVING ROOM

rug

mantel

fireplace

chair

ssock

spade

oning board

BEDROOM

light switch

pillow

mattress

bed

box of toys

BEDROOM

mover

iron

radiator

mirror

dresser

wastebasket

record player

DINING ROOM

hanging the drapes

dining table

chair

rocking chair

KITCHEN

unpacking the dishes

pans

refrigerator

stove

skateboard

27

Secret Hiding Places

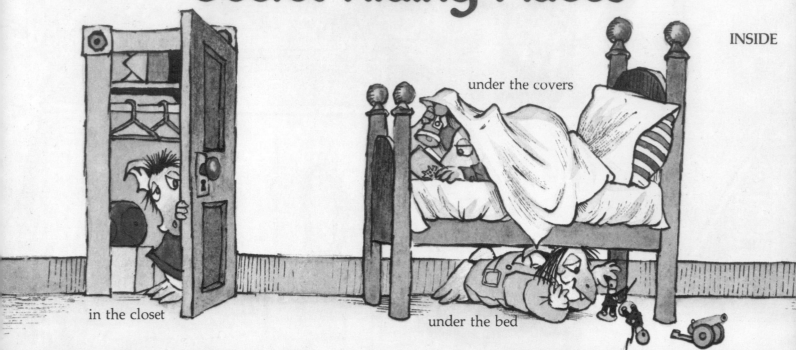

under the covers

in the closet

under the bed

behind the sofa

in the dark

in the sofa

behind the curtains

behind a chair

under a newspaper

under a lamp shade

OUTSIDE

in a bush

behind a tree

in a blanket tent

in a hollow tree trunk

behind a rock

in a cardboard
carton clubhouse

in a hole
in the ground

under the
porch steps

NOT in the
garbage can

29

lawn mower

rake

nozzle

hose

MOWING THE GRASS

RAKING LEAVES

WATERING THE FLOWERS

sponge

hedge clippers

WASHING THE CAR

pail

TRIMMING THE HEDGE

dishes

Helping

HANGING UP YOUR CLOTHES

coat hange

closet

SETTING THE TABLE

PUTTING AWAY YOUR BOOKS

head of the bed

bookcase

TYING LITTLE BROTHER'S SHOES

broom

MAKING THE BED

toy chest

CLEANING UP YOUR ROOM

foot of the bed

30

Feelings

happy   jealous   sad

selfish

sharing

greedy

mad

First Times

first letter

first fish

first A

first bull's-eye

first electric train set

first telephone call

first home run

first camp-out

first tooth
to come out

first bicycle

first puppy

33

Things to Do or Be When You Get Bigger

farmer

truck driver

firefighter

police officer

doctor

gas station attendant

baker

storekeeper

astronaut

mail carrier

skin diver

photographer

artist

author

telephone operator

34

librarian

dentist

cabinetmaker

optician

florist

bird watcher

general

veterinarian

sailor

animal trainer

waiter

magician

pilot

juggler

taxi driver

actor

actress

hobo

35

Lessons

sheet music

SINGING   PIANO

tutu

toe shoes

BALLET

tap shoes

TAP

KARATE

swimming trunks

SWIMMING

hunting cap

saddle

reins

bridle

RIDING

mask

fencing swords

chest protector

FENCING

TENNIS

tennis ball

tennis racket

net

paintbrush

canvas

SCULPTURE

POTTERY

beret

model

easel

palette

potter's
wheel

smock

VIOLIN

BAGPIPE

CLAY

sculpting
tools

PAINTING

COOKING

pan

spoon

GROWL

SNEER

BOO

apron

mixing bowl

SCARING LESSONS

37

Colors

RED

plaid

mix:
RED
+
YELLOW
ORANGE

YELLOW

stripes

mix:
YELLOW
+
BLUE
GREEN

BLUE

checks

waterfall

cave

fish

boulder

What color is: RED + BLUE ?

38

Big and Little

Big and little,
Short and tall,
Fat and thin,
And that's not all.

Crooked and straight,
Round and square,
You can see something—
But nothing's not there.

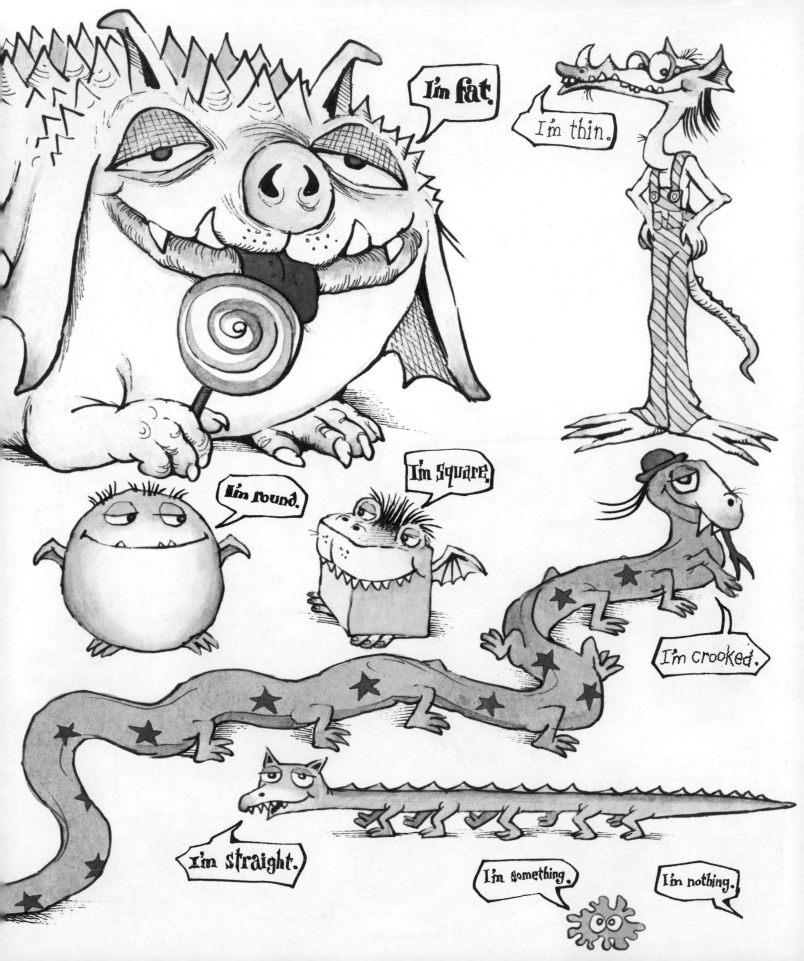

For Your Head

king's crown

toupee

moustache

queen's crown

hair ribbon

eyeglasses

sunglasses

beard

wig

football helmet

pith helmet

ponytail

chef's hat

sailor hat

baseball cap

army helmet

catcher's mask

earphones

fire fighter's helmet

makeup

POWDER

earrings

top hat

hummingbird

bonnet

42

rubbers

baseball glove

knee socks

sneakers

flippers

roller skates

boxing gloves

hiking boots

high-heeled shoes

cowboy boots

mittens

ring

high-top sneakers

wooden shoes

nail polish

sandals

argyle socks

For Your Hands and Feet

fuzzy slippers

gloves

snowshoes

rubber boots

surfboard

stilts

pogo stick

slip

dress

undershirt

under pants

belt

necktie

bow tie

suspenders

suit

vest

trousers

turtleneck

blouse

necklace

bracelet

skirt

swimming suit

swimming trunks

shirt

tank top

hula hoop

T-shirt

For Your Middle

shorts

bathrobe

45

Numbers

1 little thing

2 trollusks running

3 sleeping kerploppuses

4 peeping eyeballs

5 devils laughing

6 useless blobs

7 broken windows